Pizza Noir #3

Pizza Noir #3

Pie in the Sky

Denver Day

Other books by Denver Day

Pizza Noir #1 - Catch as Catch Can (2014)

Pizza Noir #2 - Alpha Taxonomy (2015)

Hipster Bricks - A Philosophical Novel (2016)

The Only Game in Town (2018)

Literature is art, metaphysics is aesthetic or not, this copy of *Pizza Noir #3 - Pie in the Sky* is yours to keep, and all dharma's fire. The *Pizza Noir* series is a work of fiction cut from whole cloth. None of these events occurred, and I invented the characters notwithstanding the real vigor of werewolves, homicide dicks, cold blooded killas, and space sharks.

Rev. date: May 2017

To order additional copies of the book contact:

Braswell Business Communications Services Inc.

1-518-400-2729

www.fusepowder.com

www.denverday.com

Chapters

Denver Day

Fool Me Once, Fool Me Twice...

The death at sea of officer Scott Smith of the Washington state police Tacoma bureau occurred on a Tuesday, and his funeral was set for Saturday. Pierce County personnel retrieved the body from Coast Guard custody Tuesday night. Smith was presided over by his law enforcement colleague Rick Thompson's ex-wife, the Pierce County Coroner Dixie Thompson at whose office the late state homicide investigator's stigmata had come to rest presently.

S. Smith was sharing his big sleep with a morgue full of much less peaceable creatures, to wit, the various otherworldly underwordly kinfolk of the weird furry abomination that killed the detective.

Licking his wounds meanwhile, the exhausted and fatigued Rick Thompson sat alone in his dark bedroom backlit by the flicker of old black-and-white moving pictures. His damp bones were drying out from the past two days' worth of maritime search efforts as well as from his renewed effort at recovery from alcoholism, ensuing his election to get on a wagon instead of a bender after the grisly conclusion of Smith. Thompson's condition steadied steadily.

The detective was keenly aware of the clichéd nature of the notion of a mid-career cop on the wagon. But Smith's death and other events aboard the fishing vessel *Blint Mary* had brought him nearer to an awareness about the rarity of life's elemental arrangement.

The characters in the films that illuminated his domicile committed dubious acts and mortal mistakes, and R. Thompson took comfort that their moral turpitude wasn't any skin off his back. Not so theoretically, at least.

In his recuperative solitude he was visited upon by Sandy and Kitty Licker and company, of Tacoma's Davey Jones Lickers roller derby squad. These local skaters and he had merged as fast friends in the past few weeks in the course of a local murder investigation which kept unfolding into deeper, wider, and odder scenarios than one might have reasonably anticipated.

Denver Day

A derby skater from Phoenix had her head smushed in like a volleyball in a hydraulic press, during a brawl at some roadhouse down in San Diego. At first, it was thought to be an isolated incident but some days later, vague connections with major crimes began to materialize. Namely, all along the American West Coast on the eleventh of October, dozens of strippers or nightclub dancers of various working-girl situations were slaughtered simultaneously.

Then things got really weird. As Thompson started investigating Tacoma's local edition, of wildlife so demised on October eleventh, the werewolf incidents began. Initially, all privy ears were skeptical but dark destiny refused to go easy. There was an undeniable body of evidence but it was bitterly confusing. The body count grew on a daily basis practically.

So, during the course of the investigation and its subsequent bizarro developments, Thompson befriended the local skaters. Now here they were, bearing their condolences for Smith's gory and demoralizing death. Also, Sandy and Kitty Licker brought two new associates with them, the vacationing Veronica and Becca Roller of the Phoenix Bloody Rollers derby.

Since werewolves had begun terrorizing the western U.S.A., members of the Lickers and the Rollers squads had come upon a certain preternatural effectiveness that worked against the werewolves' evil devices.

In the beginning, Thompson and Sandy

had become involved, but Sandy was rather close to the edit even for Thompson's delicate tastes. Now, the detective was seeing more of the relatively less-chaotic Kitty Licker.

So when the other women left Thompson's apartment that night, Kitty remained with him. And the next knock at Thompson's apartment door was lieutenant Danny MacKinney, the detective's division commander, who finally enjoyed the pleasure of a proper introduction to Kitty Licker.

"You break him, you buy him," MacKinney told her.

The lieutenant brought a six pack of lagers and was surprised at Thompson's polite "no thank you." But Kitty accepted one.

California state troopers had successfully delivered the bad news to Smith's next of kin, MacKinney said. He did not say more of the late Scott Smith and rightly, for there was not much useful to say at the time.

The scene in Thompson's apartment complemented the heavy weather outside. The lieutenant sat with them for a while, watching the black-and-white T.V., and Kitty's legs.

R. Thompson had seen better work days of course but he felt lucky in a number of ways, not the least of which being that he was spared a personal bifurcation at the hands of the seaborne axewielding werewolf that killed Smith.

At the time of his end, excepting the

obvious difficulties of the moment with werewolves, otherwise most notable among the late detective's caseload was the investigation of local jazz saxophonist Tina Santos' death by axe. And soon after Santos', the subsequent axe-murder-slash-rape of local musician Katherine Wells, down in Olympia only a short drive to the south, was categorically similar and probably related to the Santos killing.

Both the Santos and the Wells cases had evolved, devolved, become conflated with, or otherwise encroached darkly upon the nascent shark-and-werewolf-related carnage. And regarding the respective axe murders, both Smith's investigation and Olympia police department detective David Wallace's had begun twisting down the same nightmare fairytale rat hole as had Thompson's in the preceding weeks.

The plot went yet further south and unfortunately, the fun-house terrorscape of werewolves came to be remembered as a situation of relative peace after killer landgoing sharks darkened the Pacific Northwest's drizzly autumn. The first shark sign was encountered at the Port of Olympia Marine Terminal, where Katherine Wells' remains were discovered by longshoremen.

So by the time of his own death, Smith's investigation had worked its way up to the same if not higher levels of weird bullshit as suffered R. Thompson's who was lucky to be alive himself. Such a dark bellwether, on Thompson Smith's fate weighed heavily.

Denver Day

Zone Defense

Friday before the funeral, the people of Washington state welcomed detective Joe Lopez and sergeant of detectives Sam Carrasco of San Diego's city force. Remember, the string of troublesome events had begun with the death of Jessica Roller at a San Diego-area roadhouse, and like its peer agencies, San Diego had yet made no peace pursuant to the October eleventh stripper murders. But Carrasco and Lopez had enjoyed the privilege of meeting the good-witch derby skaters Veronica and Becca Roller, who had revisited San Diego County en route Phoenix to Tacoma.

Becca and Veronica subsequently spent

most of Wednesday through Friday training with, sleeping with, and in general assembly among their soul sisters of Tacoma's Davey Jones Lickers, and Sandy and Kitty Licker in particular. Such was their preferred mode of configuring the enemy's demise. The werewolves were mean, but also stupid and the skaters' strategy for interdiction was fairly simple. Hence, most of the Lickers' and the Rollers' time together was leisurely.

Anyway, the plan was to pick off the werewolves piecemeal as opportunity provided, until the beasts were all dead or permanently reverted to the sewers. The werewolves were hunting in pairs and living in packs so it would be most efficient to attack their dens. Sniffing them out was the only thing left to do, and it was high time.

Denver Day

Lopez and Carrasco walked into Thompson's office about lunchtime Friday. Their next stop was the diner near the station for some tea and spaghetti and bean burgers before continuing the local tour. During their meal, the investigators related to one another their body of knowledge regarding the skaters' response to the werewolves.

"I don't know if they need us or just need us to stay out of the way," Thompson said. "But our main role as peace officers is to allow them clean access to the rights of way so they can do what they gotta do."

Mulling the circumstances, they fiddled with their food.

"Would you mind taking us to the

coroner's, so we can see what the bad half looks like?" Lopez asked.

"Sure thing detective."

Coroner D. Thompson: "Some of them decay, some of them do not. All of the sharks have turned to sand," she explained, for what seemed to her like the hundredth time to tell the increasingly hopeless story. "Magic shark dust. Anyway, none of our werewolf cadavers have disintegrated, but it has been reported elsewhere. For example, the ones at the Thurston County morgue decayed despite having been shoved full of formaldehyde."

D. Thompson showed Carrasco and Lopez her ex-husband's demised suspects, Louis Ho and Keri Anders. Ho and Anders were killed during a three-way sex act with a werewolf which was the former dead hooker in whose murder Ho and Anders had been the original prime suspects. Then she showed them the late convenience store clerk Louis Xiang, and the monsters who died with him. She displayed the dusty remains of the landgoing sharks that were now helping the werewolves with their dirty work.

Come early that evening, the detectives drove over to Sandy and Kitty Lickers' place. Lopez and Carrasco were plainly giddy with the anticipation of seeing the sexy walking tarot deck who were once thought to be regular everyday derby roller skaters. The door to Sandy's apartment was open several inches already when Thompson knocked. "Come on in guys!" a voice sang out.

Veronica and Becca were half asleep in their underwear, tangled in blankets on one of the couches in the den. Women after his own habits, Thompson thought. The shower's running was audible through a bedroom door, same out of which Kitty walked and waved them toward the couch. Then she zipped into the kitchen soon returning with a tray of fresh black coffee in flesh-colored breast-shaped earthenware mugs.

"Nice ceramics, ma'am," Carrasco said, peering through his mustache at his steaming black toddy. While Kitty was up, the semi-snoozing Rollers ordered more coffee also, and Kitty happily indulged them before joining everybody on the crowded couch. They heard the shower stop and some minutes later Sandy emerged in all cotton, clean as a whistle, neat as a pin, in faded jeans and a t-shirt.

"Hello people," she smiled, sitting down by Veronica. "Are we ready to go hunting?"

All sipped coffee. The detectives drank up the abundant fleshy view of the Rollers, politely.

"We need your allowance for the civil flexibility necessary to operate," Sandy said. "Please feel free to ride with us. We will be hunting by way of our olfactories."

In their investment of such authority and confidence in a bunch of odd females, newcomers Lopez and Carrasco were mainly relying on blind faith and the benefit of the doubt. In light of his hands-on experience with them notwithstanding the ominous fate of detective Smith, Thompson (who, Carrasco reminded himself, was sleeping with at least one of these women) was quick to just say hell yes.

Anyway they were organized and mobilized. Well beyond dark about nine o'clock they headed out to the Lickers' apartment parking lot. They split up: Lopez went with Sandy in her bug; Kitty got in Thompson's unmarked sedan; and Becca and Carrasco took Carrasco's airport rental, a khaki sports-utility vehicle. Veronica rode by herself on Kitty's motorcycle. The first radio traffic was Veronica's.

"Stay in a caravan if possible. If we do split, return to the group as soon as you can. Please always stay available for contact either on the radio or the wind."

The hunting party made a northerly path on I-5 after downing plenty of tofu tacos and shakes brought to their vehicles by skatehooved carhops. The heat was on.

The Inland Inn

The women sniffed the air, tracking their quarry,

Sandy keyed her radio: "Drivers keep at a slow roll," she said. Short minutes later Veronica's voice returned.

"I got 'em," she said, "about five miles up the road, westerly, a line on three of them. I think they're asleep. They don't know we're here."

Thompson looked toward the passenger seat at Kitty who, despite the cold pouring rain, had rolled her window all the way down. Cocking her neck and squinting her eyes, she poked her head out slightly.

"She's right," she said. "All three of them are fast asleep in a motel room. This should be easy. We'll park on the opposite side of the motel lot, you guys hang back, we'll walk right in, right out. A five minute job."

Thompson's grin pierced the sedan's dimly lit vinyl interior, and she leaned over to offer a stiffened measure of velvet tongue. The detective felt himself lucky, if overwhelmed.

A blue neon sign declared the name of their location, the Inland Inn, as they approached.

The hunters were thinking as one; a collective ethical predator in search of its evil, overgrown, homicidal, sewer-dwelling rat-dog, moon-barking targets. The drivers turned off engines, switched off headlights, and hung back as the lady skaters exited the vehicles and walked off calmly. They scattered in different directions carefully making toward the other side of the property while the detectives sat waiting, watching, mindful of their sidearms.

Within about ten seconds of one another, silently the four hunters arrived at the second floor hotel room. The upstairs walkway was covered but not fully enclosed. The testy wind carried some of the rain through the fenestrated railing. The wet air glowed electric blue from the neon sign above. Veronica turned the knob, opened the door, walked in, and the others followed.

The three doomed creatures inside were

asleep in a hairy pile on the room's only bed. Gingerly, Veronica put her hand on the neck of one of the sleeping dogs. Likewise did Becca and Kitty on the other two werewolves. Together at once, they flexed grips demonstrative of their supernatural high ground, excessive pounds-on-pounds per square inch. The head of Veronica's subject severed immediately. Becca and Kitty increased their torque and off followed the other two heads. High pitched emissions sounded from the severed whelps only briefly.

The corpse of the beast killed by Veronica decomposed fully to ashes within a quarter minute. Kitty's made a crackling sound, turned into an eight-inch cockroach, flopped off the bed, and scrambled across the floor. Sandy ground it between the stained

linoleum and the bottom of her canvas high-
tops with a crackle-pop sound and a blue
flash. The room flooded with a stench like
hospital death shits and rotting flesh from
the crushed roach. The third werewolf just
laid there dead so, they carried it around
back and pitched it into a big steel garbage
bin. Sandy added some diesel from the spare
can in the boot of her bug and put that
funny kettle to the match.

In the lavatory of the motel room, they
discovered a plastic gallon jug about half full
of what was probably tap water. On the
bedside table there was a glass crack pipe,
stuffed with the charred steel of a scouring
pad; it was a tool that had been well used
although it was cool to the touch at the
moment. There were blood stains on the

bedding, werewolf menstruate evidently. There were two sets of people clothes on the floor but they found no derby uniforms, so it was not clear from which team the werewolves might have spawned or if they were ex-derby at all. Of the clothing on the floor, all pockets were devoid of any clues.

After the women and the detectives finished searching the room, Thompson considered whether he ought to call the county in for for the clean-up, but he could not really think of anything they had left unfinished, so he didn't bother. After all, when they were done with it, it was only a messy, empty, spooky hotel room, like every other.

Either the werewolves were smoking

crack, or they had eaten at least two crackheads, or, crackheads like derbiers suffered a heightened risk for ill-fated lupine transformations. Thompson figured, if the crackheads had not been devoured, otherwise fucked to death, or turned into werewolves themselves, then they were likely to return to this scene to search for crack they might've dropped because crackheads are predictable like that.

He wrote his phone number on a blank tablet on the T.V. stand. Under the paper he also slid two twenty dollar bills, to imply he was a supplier, or at least that he knew the score. Outside, the fire in the motel's garbage bin had bathed the property temporarily in a warm amber light but the blaze was fading, and the parking lot renormalized to its faint neon.

It was about ten-thirty when they left. As the weird blue ubiquity of the Inland Inn glowed in their rearview mirrors, Thompson recalled Smith's also-weird and poorly lit death scene. The werewolves at the Inland Inn reminded him of Tuesday's disaster and he wondered if any of them were involved in the battle on the deck of the doomed *Blint Mary.*

Sandy keyed up her radio: "I don't see any more nearby. Let's break and come back for more on the next shift."

Kitty looked across the front seat at Thompson, who asked in turn, "Wanna go to the bar?"

Above, as Below

R. Thompson pointed the sedan south, toward MC's Ale House where Kitty and various other Lickers were part-time staffers. MC's was swinging in anticipation of the nearing zero hour. Kitty fed the jukebox, then she and Thompson found a seat at the crowded bar. He saw Lopez, Carrasco, and the visiting Rollers darken the door a few minutes later. Or lighten it, better said. All except Thompson ordered whiskey highballs. Of the hunting party, Sandy was the only one absent.

Veronica kicked several people's asses at bar-rules pool and continued running the table against challengers. They stayed until

Denver Day

MC's closed at three, then motored back to Kitty's and Sandy's. As they were parking, Carrasco and Lopez noted the festive crowd in the courtyard commons. People were smoking, joking, drinking beer under a community patio canopy littered with anthropomorphic outdoor space heater towers whose orange glow fended off the wet cold.

The next morning about ten, the team awoke from their late autumn nap to prepare for Smith's funeral, which was set for noon. A friendly competition for the shower ensued to rinse away the moss and musk of the night before.

The funeral service for Janice Allison was set for two o'clock, so it was a double header of formalities. Allison had been accidentally killed at Kelly Sammys pub, ironically during the wake memorial for her niece Tina Santos who was the victim of record in the late detective Smith's axe-related homicide investigation.

That axe murder case was designated to Smith and not to R. Thompson in light of Thompson's recent sexual involvement with Santos. Because Allison was visiting from out of state at the time of her death, and because the late Santos was her only known family, the attendance at her service should have been lighter, probably. But since there was a topically relevant, already-dressed-for-a-funeral crowd to hand from Smith's formalities, aunt Janice's memorial went off as a popular success.

Denver Day

Anyway, Smith's rainy high-noon interment was heavily trafficked by traveling public servants in addition to the local fuzz, for example Thurston County Coroner Ben Jones and Olympia Police Detective David Wallace with whom Smith had collaborated alongside Olympia's investigation of the Katherine Wells axe murder/rape at the Port of Olympia Marine Terminal. To-date the case lacked any proper resolution and Olympia begrudgingly numbered among those communities beset with the troubles of werewolves and their land-going shark minions.

"Speaking of which," having quietly read Thompson's mind, Kitty whispered in his ear during the service, "there is activity down there as we speak: We're hunting werewolves in Olympia after the match tonight."

"Who do the Lickers have this evening?" he whispered back.

"It's the Plaiden Switches again."

After the conclusion of the rites of Smith, the group walked over to Allison's. Santos' jazz band was there, as well as the standard Kelly Sammys bartender who was on duty when Allison was impaled by the fallen swordfish mount from above the door to the pub's restrooms. Dutifully present, also were the swinging Professor Foster and his partner Daisy Wilson, the couple who had been capital parties of interest for Smith in the Santos investigation, prior to its supernatural turns leading Smith down the garden path.

Janice Allison's funeral was an exercise in

the study of the incestuousness of human acquaintances among loosely engineered happenstance. It was also a who's who of who was and who wasn't still alive amid the heightened risk for a supernaturally violent death among the lucky, and, it was a fairly sober argument about who could be next. Never twice lightning strikes?

On the way dropping off Kitty, Thompson asked her if she sensed anything weird about Foster and Wilson.

"I don't think they're bad. Maybe just bad luck," she said. "You might think of them as horny and in the way. That Thurston County coroner is a cutie though. Jones. But all of your friends from out of town seem to be on the up-and-up. Just generally speaking."

"As we are looking for trouble after the match tonight deliberately, it's worth considering whether anything is in the cards during the actual derby event," he asked.

"Demonstrably, our brains and good faith have outdone the werewolves' M.O. of evil creeping, so a natural response from them would be to avoid us. Then again, their lack of brains could also put them right at our front door at anytime, so it's not out of the question. But as of this very moment, no they are not coming. Not today and not tonight. In fact, for some reason, they are a good distance south today."

R. Thompson dropped off Kitty about four-thirty and went home for a nap before that evening's resumption of hound-on-hound affairs. Lopez and Carrasco returned to their hotel to do likewise. The plan seemed fairly straightforward. A four hour nap followed by an exciting derby event. Then a trip down to Thurston County looking for seaside werewolves. What could possibly go wrong?

Meanwhile in Olympia, B. Jones and D. Wallace discussed the disposition of the Katherine Wells rape/homicide investigation. They were experiencing the same type of moral moment as their Pierce County peers, among others, had been reckoning.

That is, the suspects were nonhuman and difficult to collar. No positive disposition through proven methods of containment availed. All preconceived notions of proper conduct in police work, and even reality, were subject to hard and irreverent looks. It could either be viewed as a total defeat or a rare career opportunity. Regardless of taxonomy, no one ever wants to be, or even meet, the pessimistic engineer.

Denver Day

The Ends

Again Veronica dreamed, as she had all her life of an endless night in a neverending wood, vexed in labyrinthine catacombs and the plummeting, dusty ramparts of a towering, forest cloaked estate.

Inhabiting this long-recurring twilight world of hers were two bipedal canines. One of them wore white coveralls, the other creature's were blue. One aided Veronica's harried escape from the dogged pursuit of the other, but the polarity of the beings' allegiance alternated relentlessly and Veronica was ever in the breach. She could never rest as any respite or quarter was fleeting, and frequently the switch happened within earshot of both creatures. Hence, from the warden of the moment as well, the dreamer had learned to also keep a safe distance which allowed her a crucial few seconds' head start.

After hours of dreaming time, which could amount to an in-dream measure of months and more, the result was always the same. Chase time varied but she always felt like she was being toyed with, since the pursuits seemed to take longer than necessary.

These dreams began when Veronica was very small, as far back as she could remember. If not eaten on a given night, she could easily count on it the next, when the cycle continued. She was always caught and devoured, sooner or later. Sometimes her soul would survive an ending and she would start awake safely in bed, relieved, but hesitant to resume sleep. Sometimes she was just returned to some position in the infinite loop either deep in the forest, or somewhere in the manor, or in the stables, or about the tended fields...

Such was her dreaming reality every night forever, until tonight when its meaning became clear. Several days after a gruesome late-night traffic accident on some lonesome Arizona highway, which had transformed the Phoenix Bloody Rollers derby team into minor wolf goddesses, Dusty and Rainy Roller had become lost at sea during a werewolf hunt. This time they died along with the erstwhile crew of the *Blint Mary,* off the coast of Washington state, after the fishing vessel was attacked by seaborne werewolves. The Coast Guard had found the boat, drifting crewless but for carcasses; detective Smith was later killed on the same ship after it had been commandeered to trawl for werewolves.

"Veronica it's Dusty," her dream's current warden spoke. In her mind's eye, Veronica saw the two Rollers standing on a high balcony with a spiral of stone stairs descending behind them into a salty darkness. They were near ocean, the taste was in the air. She looked toward the sea view beyond the railing. After she woke, she still heard the breakers.

Also R. Thompson's nap ended. In his

dream he heard the voice of Scott Smith. "I'll be right back," he said. It was unmistakably Smith's voice. Then the dream cut to an open ocean, calm and starlit.

Come seven-thirty Saturday evening, pursuant to the season and the weather, it had been dark for two hours. Thompson showered quickly and hit the door for the Lickers home track. From their hotel, Carrasco and Lopez made the same way.

The plain-clothed detectives met in the parking lot where Thompson, about two or three melees ago, encountered his first phantasmagoric werewolf battle.

The atmosphere was requisitely electric and beery. They walked in together and found a seat in the tattooed bleachers featuring derby aficionados from many walks of life. It was a melting pot of coffeehouse emos, skateboarders, punks, delegates of trashy new money, off-duty blue shift, college kids, et al.

Preferred Lickers antagonist, the Seattle Plaiden Switches derby was on hand in leggy, tartan glory. Thompson could see Patchy Plaiden, with whom he'd shared a bed at Sandy's and Kitty's and given a ride back up to Renton, the morning after the Switches' previous visit. She was a cute dirty blonde, smallish, and an excellent skater.

He wondered if Patchy experienced the transformation that so many of her peers had. Or she may have been already illuminated like that, but their introduction had occurred before the detective's own development of eyes for such things. So he watched her stretch with an eye for that subtle aura.

He could see it on her and many other skaters, even in the visible spectrum. The detective was realizing that all people, given the proper tinkering and proximity with the likes of these women, could achieve such a heightened measure of being. For example, the new sensitivity was helping him as a criminal investigator, particularly because he was detecting, more often than not, literal monsters nowadays. Anyway, it was plain to see now, Patchy was a rainbow.

Lopez and Carrasco were getting a kick out of the derby match. It was a tight one prevailing the Plaiden. For good measure, Thompson and Lopez had stepped out for a few looks during play breaks, but no bloody fiasco recurred.

As far as Thompson was concerned, the end of times was turning out much pleasanter, though he'd grant you also much weirder, than any of his previous notions entertained pursuant to the matter. So far. Still, real fire and brimstone was threatening, and a safe presumption was of more to come.

But for attributing the new reality to some tributary function of the apocalypse, there was no other supporting mythos to underwrite the late and local mystical events. Definitely, it was the end insofar as it had changed reality, drastically and permanently, for the detective and his colleagues. He reflected gratefully that as far as he knew, he had so far survived.

Sunken Lantern

By eleven o'clock the three detectives, two Lickers, and Patchy were southbound on I-5, with three in front and three in the rear of Thompson's unmarked Crown Vic. Carrasco asked how come the ad hoc visiting Rollers had been absent during Lickers v. Plaidens. Apparently, they had gone on some special assignment, Sandy explained:

"Veronica woke up from a dream this afternoon with a bee in her bonnet about Dusty and Rainy Roller. They're headed south tonight too, in my bug."

Sandy and Patchy's ears perked up as Ricky Thompson's radials whirred against the highway. Sandy, who was riding shotgun, potted down the dash radio, leaned over, tilted her head, and looked west.

Meanwhile passing through Olympia, Veronica Roller redirected Sandy's little diesel back into a northerly trajectory as they made their way up the east shore of Budd Inlet. Becca Roller switched off the AM radio. "Sandy and Kitty and their boyfriends are on their way out of Tacoma," she said. "Hmmm."

Driving from Tacoma to Olympia takes thirty minutes. Up Budd Inlet to the light at Dofflemeyer Point takes another twenty and that's where Veronica and Becca went in no apparent hurry. In the area of Boston Harbor Marina, Veronica switched off the engine and the two women sat silently together in the car for another five more minutes before taking the short walk to the light. They accepted the acquittal offered by the melodious surf and sat, looking out over the foggy water.

Fifteen minutes later, the subjects of their pick-up approached. Two figures walked toward them from the water. Wet, lean, dark, beautiful creatures striped and illumined sublimely amidst the hypnotizing fluidity of the waves. Becca and Veronica stood, turned, and began walking back to the Volkswagen without looking back, and the two sirenes followed. The Rollers got back in the car, and some moments later let the passengers into the backseat. V. Roller restarted the motor and wheeled it back to the main road.

The heat from the little diesel block was circulating into the cab through the dash vents. The door windows were cracked about half an inch to keep the windshield from fogging up. There was quiet excepting wind noise and the rhythmic rumble of the engine. Four warm, alive, comfortable, grateful people feeling but not talking, making their way briskly down the highway. Still neither of the girls in the front looked into the back.

As they approached Olympia it was Dusty Roller who finally spoke. Becca turned around and Veronica looked into the rearview mirror beholding their rescued teammates. The two born-again Rollers were bright eyed, bushytailed, and no worse for the infinite wear of their late deep-blue journey.

"Hey you guys are a sight for sore eyes," came Dusty's standard rasp.

"For crying out loud," Becca scolded, "y'all have to be more careful. Should I even ask?"

Rainy fielded the question. "The last thing I remember, we were on a fishing vessel, in a skirmish with a hive of outrigging werewolves. Never mind now how that all came to pass, but anyway. At first we were drowning them one after another but then somehow they attacked us with demon sharks. For them to be able to control sharks or even try to, the werewolves must be evolving. And watch out for those crazy fish, man. They may be stupid but they pop out of nowhere. I was gored by an out-ofphase shark and I didn't even see it coming. That's the last thing I remember. Next thing I knew, we were walking up to you guys back there on the shore. How long have we been gone?"

Southbound also meanwhile, Thompson's vehicle crossed the Olympia city limits making way to Kelly Sammys pub. He parked and they skittered through the drizzle into the establishment that was glowing with its usual bustle. Particularly in this setting, it was noticeable that the girls were somehow different. In the absence of daylight their eyes grew large as dinner plates, their ears flattened back, lengthened, and pitched moving shadows. They were frisky from their evening skate, the weather, and their fulfilled precognition of Dusty's and Rainy's rejoin.

Next entering the pub, Kitty's and Sandy's eyes swept naturally to a booth near the bar where the four Rollers were sitting. They added several loose chairs in order to cram everybody around the table. First the Phoenix girls were introduced to the dishy Patchy Plaiden, then the Lickers executed an esoteric ritual with Dusty and Rainy.

"You guys have been way down below the ocean," Sandy smiled.

"I think so. We don't remember being gone but we consider ourselves lucky," Dusty said, returning a warm smile. An array of oily bean burgers, colorful veggie tacos, and bubbling, shadowy, brewed concoctions settled onto the table. Accordingly the lost Rollers were welcomed back among the living.

Sunday morning R. Thompson's phone rang around ten-thirty. The area code was local but he didn't recognize the number. He set aside his cold cereal and answered.

"Hello?" a voice on the other end croaked.

"Yes hello," he said, nonchalant.

A few moments of silence, then a man's voice, "Hey, uh, I, found the number you left at the Inland Inn motel up on I-5."

The verbal exchange was between two men but the detective felt the caller was not alone. Thompson led the dance from there. "So, ahh, are you guys OK?" he fished.

"Good, good...we're good," the caller said. "You got anything I need?"

"I do," the detective replied. The character on the other end of the line provided his location: a nearby motel, different though surely no less respectable, than the Inland Inn.

Brunch

R. Thompson pulled into the parking lot of the motel about a half hour after the phone call from the stranger. He parked, stepped out, leaned against his vehicle, and studied the outward appearance of the building. It was only one story, with all of its domiciles facing the highway. It had the feel of a trailer park, or perhaps a barracks.

The rain had let up although the sky still threatened. A few miles away there was a thunder clap. In one of the windows the blinds rustled, the door opened, and a lanky but stout male walked out. There was a ponytail protruding from under his skullcap, his jacket was without patches or insignia,

and the leather looked new. The man was
not a tweaking crack or meth addict, which
the detective had expected in light of the
ominous debris at the Inland Inn.

They sized each other up, and the
prevailing normality generated fresh cause for
suspicion on the part of both parties. It was
a pretty low bar by all accounts, and the
unknown biker's expectations were not
generally positive either. Rain began to fall
and the stranger motioned at the open door.

"Wait a minute. Do you have a name?"
Thompson asked.

"Yeah," the man answered, "it's Crimson.
I'm B.A. Crimson." A short minute later
Thompson was glad he had asked.

The man walked inside and the detective

followed him. Once Thompson cleared the threshold, Crimson ducked, spun, and delivered a roundhouse kick to his midsection. The detective saw it coming and was able to bend and block, but he still took a glancing blow. Thompson rolled, guarding his head and ribs. If the kick had been higher he probably could have ducked it entirely, and probably could have skipped right back out the open door, but the inertia of his evasive action had moved him in a different direction.

In any case, at the unmistakable clatter of a pump-action shotgun, their brief scuffle came to a full stop. Crimson bounced to his feet. Thompson froze and looked up to see the weapon covering him in the hands of a woman. Her eyes were clear and willing. She kicked the door closed and there followed a perilous silence.

The detective gently cleared his throat. Wary of any more kicks or punches, he moved his eyes slowly from her glare to Crimson, who glowered like a brick tower. Then the woman spoke. "Who are you?"

But her summary judgment was still pending and she didn't yet lower the twelve gauge. Thompson considered his pistols, one on his ankle and the other in a shoulder holster under his coat.

"Thompson," he answered her, carefully motionless.

"What's your business?"

"I am investigating a murder," he said. "I can understand your caution."

"What happened at the Inland Inn last night?" she prodded.

Thompson's eyes met hers which were still unfriendly. "Do you mind if I go ahead and sit at that table?" he asked, but she didn't answer.

So keeping his hands up in plain sight and careful to keep facing the woman he slid over very slowly. He sat at the table. She lowered the barrel some, taking a slightly less aggressive posture but still threatening. Her eyes didn't change.

"What's your stake in this stretch of highway?" Thompson asked her, but Crimson answered.

"I heard through the grapevine about some...well...some "unusualities" going on out here, that's what."

Before the ruckus, as soon as Crimson had given his name, Thompson knew immediately who the man was. William Alan Crimson had made parole (under the conditions of which, no doubt, playing at or near shotguns was a violation). B.A. Crimson had been at the Arizona state farm on a rape and murder rap, and his little brother William Robert Crimson, was twenty-three when he was shot to death by Becca Reaugh (Becca Roller) during a domestic dispute in Scottsdale.

Veronica (Martinez) Roller, meanwhile, was involved with B.A.'s prosecution before her retirement from the Navajo Nation police. Becca and Veronica met during the adjudication of B.A.'s case, and after completing her own ADC bid, Becca moved in with Veronica.

How did this freebird relate to the local "unusualities?" The man must know those girls are out here, Thompson thought. And with their keen second sight, they probably know he's here too. Of all the times for B.A. Crimson to be trawling around up here, why now? Maybe he really wasn't on parole...

Of course, the detective also wondered at the woman with the shotgun and at how fate, or the Rollers, or whatever, had placed him in the delicate position of reuniting these statutorily odd bedfellows.

"You know Veronica and Becca are out here, right?" the detective came to the point flatly. The conversational twist put Thompson back on a more fair footing with his new acquaintances.

Sunday after lunchtime, the houseful of Lickers, Rollers, and a Plaiden were rising and shining at Sandy's and Kitty's. They had reached a consensus that the San Francisco Bay Area was a hub of werewolf activity, and the wayfinding dialog occurring since Dusty's and Rainy's revival had reinforced the hunters' compulsion to visit California.

Kitty fielded a call from R. Thompson, who asked her to hand the phone to V. Roller. After about a minute of listening, Veronica hung it up.

"Oh well oh well oh well. Rick the Dick

has Bill Crimson up at some motel on I-5," she said, "with some woman who's probably his new parole officer wife."

"Wow," Becca said. "At least he's re-entering the world on our side of the fray, but know this: I'm not taking any shit off that motherfucker. Not for historical matters, or new business, or otherwise."

"Nobody's taking it and nobody's dishing it out. Don't worry about it," Veronica said. "Still water runs the deepest, and blessed be the ties that bind, and he's either for us or against us, and shall I go on? It's a moot point anyway; I think he's here to help. But I'll read him the same riot act in a few minutes because we're going to meet them, right now."

Sometimes Old Habits Die Easy

The four Rollers piled into the bug and made way for the diner across the street from R. Thompson's office to rendezvous with the detective's latest odd catch. He had figured that location to be as neutral and safe as any for a potentially toxic reunion.

The onset of supernatural hubbub seemed to have the same chilling effect on parolees and parole officers as it had on police and undertakers. And, Veronica had guaranteed him the meeting would be civil, and he did have substantial faith in her ability to keep the peace.

Meanwhile, on Crimson's bike he and his

rider followed behind Thompson. As they passed by it, the Inland Inn beckoned to them with its neon blue glow.

The Rollers were already within, seated at a booth. As their long-lost acquaintance and his lady associate, and R. Thompson approached them, Veronica and Becca stood up. There were no handshakes, but common respect for the golden rule was definitely in play.

Recall that Becca killed Crimson's brother, and Veronica was his arresting officer in the case that bought him hard time at the Arizona state farm. And now, the man had the cojones to violate multiple conditions of his parole by leaving the state to seek an audience with these same women.

Extraordinary and rarely tractable excuses for such an act might include leaps of faith, force majeure, outright foolishness, or, werewolf induced cataclysm.

Crimson was mindful of his awkward position, surely, so it was a relief for him (and for Dick Thompson) when the shiny women took his presence more or less in stride, under the circumstances, and greeted him as the old family friend that he technically was.

"Hello Bobby," said Veronica, the first to speak after everyone was seated, "how long have you been out?" (Referring to both of the brothers as Bobby was an old saw among friends of the Crimsons, apparently.)

"About two months. Thanks for the

summons."

"Thank you for coming. You're gonna be alright, Bobby Crimson," she said.

Veronica and Becca introduced Dusty and Rainy who, in their state of being freshly re-assimilated, were glowing like the sun. The four Rollers swirled and glowed, forever changing the realities of B.A. and his state-issued girlfriend.

Several V.L.V.M.T.P.s (very large veggie-mongo taco plates) were ordered, and for twenty minutes the party gorged deliberately with little, if any, speech beyond "pass the hot sauce."

Crimson eventually explained that he had attended the derby match in Phoenix between the Flagstaff squad and the Bloody Rollers, reports of whose results were conflicting and so much contested historically, as certain local authorities swore that either one or both teams went missing after the match. However some fans said neither team showed up in the first place meanwhile others said they witnessed the full event and had even reported a final score. Crimson's account supported the latter more optimistic version, that both teams played hard including Rollers Veronica, Becca, Dusty, and Rainy.

"But there was something weird, and it was the first of many events that have led me out here to see you all. I could tell there was something different about the skaters. Their bodies were plainly glowing. I don't know who else noticed but it was obvious to me."

"There have been some scarier things also. That night we saw stuff in the parking lot, and on the highway coming home, and even in local bars. Now, I've seen fearsome things in my time but nothing like this before."

"Look, Bobby, this is why we contacted you," Veronica said. "We knew you were there that night, and we also know you've seen what we're up against. These are important things, what you've witnessed so far, and you can help us. Don't worry, we will prevail. So, come south with us, we're taking a ride to the Bay Area on I-5. Leaving today and arriving tomorrow, for the purpose of werewolf hunting."

Carrasco and Lopez joined the caravan,

since they were due to return to California anyway; With them as properly sworn officers in the mix, chief detective Sam Wilson of the Oakland Police Department might feel better about giving a key to the city to a gaggle of derby skaters and at least one parolee, notwithstanding their recently more favorable position among the pecking order of whosits and ne'er-do-wells.

Denver Day

Firecrackers

Making adieus to Carrasco, Lopez, and the rest of his colorful new acquaintances, R. Thompson called it quits for the evening. Under the cover of a cold rain he stole away to his apartment for a twenty-four-to-thirty-six-hour weekend of solitary R&R in his cluttered but peaceful domicile (pending temporary quietude in Tacoma, which was entirely possible since so many of the city's noisiest characters were piping their hubbub down to The Golden State.)

But first, he stopped by the station and telephoned Sam Wilson, chief detective of the Oakland police, to warn him that a foray of well-meaning weirdos was coming down on his ass sometime tomorrow. Thompson and Wilson had been collaborating on the October eleventh homicide investigations and the ensuing werewolf misadventures. Wilson and his personnel had seen and experienced much of the same weirdness as Tacoma, so the man was cooperative and sympathetic.

Thompson explained the new developments with the derby and what kind of support they needed for urban werewolf tracking. He reassured Wilson that it appeared to be easy work for the women and that there was no need for him to be overly concerned.

"We are lucky to have them on our side," the detective reassured him. "The werewolves are a road hazard, and they say you have a cluster of them in your backyard. These women read it on the wind, and they're hellbent for leather."

"I guess I don't have any choice," Wilson said, sounding resigned. After he hung up, the Oakland chief warned his lieutenants of more incoming weirdness.

R. Thompson took a long Sunday evening nap. In the small hours, after her shift at M.C.'s, Kitty's knock at his apartment door woke him. They enjoyed their usual black-and-white cops-and-robbers film with popcorn and exchanged massages to work out the muscle kinks inflicted upon them by the day's living. Et cetera. The rain continued.

"You want to go do a quick job on some werewolves?" she asked, "just me and you."

"Now? Really?" It was three-forty-five.

"I wouldn't insist if they weren't so close," she argued. "Anyway it won't take long. Then I'll take care of whatever you want for breakfast, and I'll wait on you hand and foot all day."

That solved it for the detective, so they hopped into his sedan and drove about five city blocks to a storage facility on the edge of a nearby commercial district. Two werewolves had been holed up for about forty-eight hours in one of the units, Kitty said.

"I wonder who rents storage space to actual werewolves?" Thompson asked.

"Right, well, this world takes all kinds, and there is a black market for this business, or, they could be squatting. People aren't supposed to live in these things, but you know they do," she said.

They parked the vehicle in a lot at the front of the property, carefully went over the fence, and walked quietly to the target location.

"This vertical door only locks from the outside, with a padlock, but it's not secured. Go stand in those shadows over there, and cover me while I knock. Then I'll step back, and when they come out, I'll hit them with a big blue energy ball."

He obeyed, retreating into shadows some ten yards back, drawing his pistol and training it on the entrance of the storage unit. Kitty walked over, gave five solid knocks with a fist, and backed off about fifteen paces. There were twenty seconds of quiet before a metallic creaking was heard as the door began coming slowly up.

Nothing emerged immediately, and only darkness could be seen from Thompson's position. Then suddenly Kitty began to glow. The air around her gathered a charge that looked like a thick cloud of tiny blue lightning.

With that, the whole row of storage units was illuminated in blue daylight. They could see the two werewolves, crouched defensively, one against the back wall and the other a few feet closer to the door.

Kitty's ionized turquoise aura gathered up a snappy bright current, then flashed white with a sharp crack. The local physical space seemed to warp, including the area occupied by the structures and the pavement. A pulse arced from Kitty's outstretched palm, and grounded out through the nearest werewolf.

The creature was cooked as it closed the circuit on Kitty's blue current. Then Kitty charged up again and hooked up the other one. When she switched off the first one and lit up the second, the first stayed momentarily vertical with its fur smoking, then it started to flash, pop, and crackle. When she unhooked the second monster it began to smoke and fizz, as the first one exploded into a swirl of amber and lavender flames.

Adventures On Parole

Crimson and the missus, the four visiting Rollers, and the two San Diego detectives began their journey south on Interstate 5 about dark-thirty Sunday. Like Thompson, Sandy and Kitty took a mulligan.

Somewhere near the California-Oregon border the travelers took respite at a truck stop. Some showered, some exercised, some copied a few ZZZs, and they all ate.

The story of Crimson's mysterious woman who did not talk much, became clearer during their six hours at the truck stop. Lydia Chapel.

Chapel had taken an institutional interest

in Crimson's community re-entry and welfare during his parole process. She was a prison reform activist and a victim advocate for the Arizona criminal court.

Her personality enabled deep, charismatic devotion to her work and to her clients in all of her cases, and when she and Crimson fell in love it engendered a powerful chemistry. Their future was bright and their collective past was a formidable education for their now-coupled spiritual inertia. The S.N.A.F.U. of them bungling into werewolves further enabled their campaign of original and unfettered self-righteousness. Their gods had deposited them at the doorstep of a mysterious and challenging adventure which they were not equipped to reject.

Before all returning to the highway, Veronica went over the new attack plan while the travelers re-breakfasted. The werewolves operated in small groups, often couples as exampled at the Inland Inn (and at the storage facility). They were entirely nocturnal creatures that could minimally integrate socially only with some of the darkest and seediest of society's night-walkers.

About noon, the hunting party arrived at the Oakland area. The first order of business was meeting with chief detective Sam Wilson of the Oakland police. Bearing Rick Thompson's best regards, they caught up to Wilson at a diner near Oakland Inner Harbor. Thompson had done a fair job of explaining to chief Wilson what he might expect from his visitors, so the short meeting at the diner had a straight-to-business nature.

The hunters knew exactly where the werewolves were, making for a softer sell to the local police about plans for that night's detail. Chief detective Wilson threw in with the expedition, on Loop 880 south en route to a rave party at Raiders Stadium. The scene was a who's who of pushers and the vice squad, and a general nightmare scenario for community leaders and common family interests. It follows that large-scale nighttime festival gatherings are ideal for werewolves to blend right in and prey on regular pukes; upon learning that they were going to a rave, Wilson was glad he had worn leather.

There were plenty of old crusty types in the mix but the crowd was young overall. The demographic availed numerous obvious examples of kids who were not legally adults, as well as, plenty of people in their twenties not to be trusted with much regardless of their civil status. It was not the college crowd. Not even aspiring circus crowd, at least not in a good way.

Bottom. The drop outs. A big percentage were here to take hard pharmaceutical drugs i.e. mollies, which can be used as a pill for hospice on the scratch, and the abuse of which has lasting physiological consequences. With countless additional hazards to hand, the location befitted predation.

Back in Tacoma, Thompson and Kitty

Denver Day

enjoyed a nice lunch after sleeping in a restful night. A witness to Kitty's facile organic electrical engineering, the detective was sold on the idea of deputizing the entire Lickers squad. Her natural bioelectrical weaponry suggested a simple solution to a problem he had not expected to resolve.

After she had blistered that storage area, the sheriff's office had fetched up the two werewolf carcasses and taken them to Dixie Thompson's body locker. After lunch, Kitty and Thompson went to see them.

Dead werewolves had shown a tendency to revitalize regardless of the flashiness of their demise, of course, and D. Thompson was aware of the pesky tendency. The ankles and wrists of her new wards were shackle bound.

These particular ones were not wearing uniforms bearing their derby nicknames, so their identification might have been less precise than it was with the others. There were telltale tattoos, however, and also Kitty was in a position to make educated guesses. Hear, hear, ladies and gentlemen, the late and former Ginny Rater and Butter Beaver of the Chino Wheeled Beavers derby.

"It won't be long before the world is plain out of Wheeled Beavers," said the detective.

"This bothers me some," Kitty said. "Because what if the curse sets upon another squad once the Beavers are gone?"

Death Rave

To an untrained eye, the salty crowd of ravers looked like a typical, festival-sized gaggle of stoned humanoids doing business as various neo- and post-modsters from the disco, techno, hippy, beat, and waver demographics et al. Anyway the unsuspecting and theoretically consenting adult would be right in making such categorical assumptions about the crowd. But because of tonight's werewolf action, there was a hidden depth to the assembly.

"They're here, I count seven. We'll put a tail on them and observe for a while. And don't spook them; please be inconspicuous," instructed Veronica. "Keep in mind that more could show up, come the witching hour. In good time, and definitely whenever one is about to take a civilian, go ahead and pick her off. All told, this won't take long. Everyone be cool and try to enjoy yourselves."

So that's how four off-duty derby skaters, the deputy chief of O.P.D.'s bureau of investigations, a fresh parolee and his consorting civil servant, and two San Diego P.D. grunts came to stand flatfooted in the Raiders Stadium parking lot amid thousands of morons on harsh hallucinatory pharmaceutical club drugs that night. Certainly many additional stupid activities were also afoot.

"Man, these people are dirty," Carrasco

said. "The older I get, the grosser this gets."

"Welcome, boys and girls, to the world of the living," V. Roller smiled.

By the by, Sam Wilson dutifully absorbed his initial dose of enchanted derby skaters.

They all split up to cover more ground, each sub-group being led by one of the Bloody Rollers. Wilson went with Veronica; Chapel and Crimson went with Becca. Rainy took Carrasco and Lopez, and Thompson paired with Dusty. All tactical communications were made on the wing so there was no need for radio traffic. The third shift was in full effect.

The V. Roller and Wilson detachment was the first to make contact with a wolf, in a bathroom stall with a woman who was moments from being eaten alive when Veronica kicked down the vanity door.

The werewolf was already down in the floor under the wall of the stall, slithering toward its would-be victim. The unsuspecting woman on the deuce became aware simultaneously of the furry monster at her feet and of the violent in-smashing of the stall door. It was not a peaceful shit for the fat lady. She had few options for evasive action, beyond clumsily skittering out of the stall with her pants around her ankles, and that she did with impressive spirit.

Veronica grabbed the prostrate monster by the legs and dragged it from the stall. She ducked as it stood up and let fly with a haymaker. Wilson broke leather and covered, but before he could shoot, Veronica instantiated a rising, sharp scream that caused the beast to burst into billowing teal-colored flames.

The monster screeched with earsplitting madness as it struggled futilely against the magic deployed upon it. Chief Wilson shielded his eyes and backed off. He holstered his heater but kept a hand close to it. Then, the Roller wolf emitted a skittering hiss like a cat's, and the flaming monster escalated into a hot, bright, white burn. A report followed, loud as a high powered rifle, then the lighting in the room normalized. Where the thing had been, only the light, fresh scent of sandalwood and a scorch mark remained.

"How's that for incense, chief?" she smiled at Wilson. He did not have anything to say, but he was profoundly relieved.

The witnesses in the lavatory were also speechless, and the near-victim was long gone. Roller and Wilson exited the restroom.

"We just snuffed one of 'em in the shitter," Veronica said. "She was about to cherry pick some gal from under the wall of a toilet stall. Add that approach to known vectors."

From some undisclosed location within the Oakland-Alameda County Coliseum, Wilson heard Dusty say "roger that."

Denver Day

Air Support

It was about midnight. The next pick-off involved snappy work by Becca Bloody Roller in an elevator. Right before it wolverized a small handful of young female ravers, she dispatched it with cold white lightning from her fingertips. When the doors of the lift opened on the ground floor, Chapel and Crimson were there to behold a frozen, shattered, demised monster while the near-victims fled without looking back. Becca stepped out and gestured at the deceased beast which then vanished, leaving behind only a light and quickly dissipating patchouli-flavored smoke.

One by one, the leisurely effort by the

Rollers and their deputies greased all of the actual werewolves at the coliseum. The last couple of beasts were slightly more challenging to dispatch because, by then, a few of the land-going sharks had manifested and were passively assisting the werewolves. What looked like it was going to be an easy night's work became somewhat more complex, but it could have been worse and luckily it was quickly resolved.

In their strange relationship with the werewolves, the sharks were arguably more mysterious because their nature and origins were even less clear. The skaters' theory was that the sharks' faculty was compromised, enabling the werewolves' control of them. Anyway, their exact role and relationship became more obvious that night.

Denver Day

There were only two werewolves left at the stadium, paired up, having finally sensed the end-run unfolding on them. The hunting party was gathered back together for the cinch. Hereupon, Dusty and Rainy spotted shark sign.

There were forms looking nearly humanoid, lurking in the shadows and crevices near the werewolves; appearing as sort of trout-faced persons and, at a glance, reasonable enough to pass for some average random dude encountered on a crowded street. Beyond a blush, however, their numbers and state were in flux. There would be several, then only one, then again a handful. And they seemed to be cloaked in some type of iridescent, insubstantial, briny nether-garments. The sharks were shoaling about the local metaphysical terrain, and to lend them one's focused attention further belied their alien nature, evoking their luminous blue-turquoise bodies.

After Dusty zapped and fried the stadium's penultimate werewolf, several of the deep-blue devils manifested in a zone defense perimeter around the last dog standing. The watery shadow figures began to make darting rapid-fire lunges at the hunters.

So as the second-to-last werewolf boiled in swirling polychromatic flames, Dusty redirected her attention to the last one. Soon also it exploded into a glorious plasmatic orb, incidental to which the land-going sharks were released from some invisible fetter. At that point, the shark's lupine altruism seemed to pass. They stopped hiding too. They were broad-daylight visible, and they were everywhere, and with much pleasanter countenances.

That was all relatively good news even for a rave party; but about five minutes later the hunters and essentially everyone else in the stadium were further surprised, grandly so. First, there was a subtle vibration that grew plainer until every damn elementary particle in the local context vibrated in response. All molecules jiggled amid the people, the walls, the local atmosphere, and everywhere in between. Then came the glow, not from above but from everywhere. Shine, all around, behind, underneath, in every direction. Like the smell of spilled gasoline, the ethereal light saturated the scene. In a few more minutes, the vibration throttled back to a subtler meter. Stoned loudmouths notwithstanding, the venue was anachronistically placid as the crowd strained to hear the quietening of the effervescent energy source. The non-linear glow shifted from a somewhat harsher higher band, to a mellower sun-colored range as the vibration softened.

Rainy poked Dusty in the ribs as they looked up to observe an event of interest in the sky. With an instinctive respect, the gazes of all people in the venue turned upward, beholding with some astonishment the contents of the air above.

It was a mother ship, and its appearance

Denver Day

was capital in comparison with any and all other local physical objects or celestial bodies. This cigar was the sharks' mama. The space fish skittered, floated, flipped, danced, spun, and tarried at various speeds, in groups of many sizes and arrangements, as they disappeared into the skirts of the craft. Then, along with all of her sharks, the vessel was gone.

Veni, Vidi, Sharkey

The grand finale at Raiders Stadium turned the bothersome apocalyptic weirdness of the West Coast werewolf affair into an intergalactic superbejesus shitshow.

"Well, it does explain the sharks," Wilson said, reporting back to his colleague in Tacoma.

At the other end of the line, Thompson chuckled. "Oh yeah, space sharks of course. I nearly forgot."

It was mid-Tuesday morning. After dispatching all werewolves at the stadium followed by the sharky U.F.O. business, there was little else left to do except lay down and dream of it all.

"Yeah. Anyway also, I believe the skater ladies gained some new insight last night, but they will have to give you the details themselves," Wilson continued. "I hear they are staying down here for one more night."

"Well last night sounds like a hard act to follow," Thompson said, "I hope this spaceship shit does not escalate. I think."

"But you know it will."

The four Rollers huddled, mulling their progress, the current state of affairs, and potential paths ahead.

The briefing comprised Dusty, Rainy, Veronica, Becca, Chapel, and Crimson, around a lunch spread at some vegan dish in view of the Golden Gate. Earlier that morning, officers Carrasco and Lopez started back to San Diego, and Wilson went to work.

"Beyond affirming what we know and what we do not," Veronica posited, "we must fathom consideration of what we don't know we don't know, and what we can't know, in order to weigh the undefined. All at once."

The werewolf interloping had begun with the Beaver's bus in the Bay, and since those particular monsters had now all managed to get themselves refried or decapitated or otherwise zeroed, the rave was the end of the line for the undead Chino Wheeled Beavers.

"And as we observed when Dusty plugged the last Wheeled Beaver wolf, the landgoing starfaring sharks all are freebirds now," V.

Roller remarked. All nodded.

"Anyway, I have contemplated the matter further and here's the deal. Who or whatever is causing the undead werewolf mobilization on this continent is doing it elsewhere also, or at least from elsewhere. And what I mean by elsewhere is," she went on, discretely pointing at the sky, "well, you know. *Boldly* distant. *Far* away. Above as below. The long and the short of it is, that the werewolves represent an interstellar vector capable of subverting collateral minions like alien marine life."

"And that's a rub. Bearing in mind the relationship between space sharks and werewolves, we can triangulate which star systems are "occupied," therefore, we can also map the very extra-terrestrial influence that mutated the Chino Beavers," Veronica explained. "So, in areas in or out of the galaxy, where star sharks are light as a feather, we might expect to find no occupying werewolves. It follows, that where sharks or other local system species are compromised however, then something is probably wrong. We'll detect and respond; it's no different than what we are already doing here, practically. This is a bull market."

Crimson blinked. V. Roller's objective assessment was not a surprise under the circumstances but it did generate some fantastic discussion, and the ambitious analysis further defined their present work content as that of actual superheroes, for better or worse.

But Can We Get There From Here?

There was no guarantee against further untimely lupine mutations, despite recent observations in support of the theory that the death of the last Wheeled Beaver emancipated all local space-going sharks.

The hunters of the derby estimated that astronomical mapping would be useful, and that other species might be similarly susceptible to the recent problems on earth. They spent the rest of Tuesday thinking about astral travel.

Chapel and Crimson slept off their road weariness and late-night U.F.O. exhaustion at the hotel. The couple were in no way as supernaturally charged as their white-witch travel companions, but the derby luck was starting to rub off on them.

Meanwhile, all was quiet in Tacoma. Still raining, and still quiet. Beautiful and worthwhile as the derby girls were, and are, the fact of the visiting Bloody Rollers being on hiatus in California made for calmer waters in Washington state. But nothing lasts forever.

Tuesday afternoon, Thompson's phone rang. It was his ex-wife.

"Hey Rick."

"Dixie what have you."

"I don't think our werewolves will be coming back. Not this time. I've even called off the morgue guards we had posted."

Denver Day

"What gives?"

"It's like a spell has been broken. Their hyper-evolved canine attributes are gone now. The bodies are reflecting their actual pre-transformation instances of death, which by the way for Ginny Rater and Butter Beaver amounts to fairly fresh casseroles; Ginny and Butter did not go peacefully, and their remains have the buckshot and hatchet wounds to show for it. Oh, and all of the shark dust, that hadn't already disappeared, is gone now."

"We never say never, doc, but that all sounds like good news. And you know damn well that this situation is still dicey. Some of the girls went werewolf hunting last night, successfully, in San Francisco. Maybe the unraveling of the corpses back into normal stiffies is a consequence of their success. But, I worry that their hunt will just open the door for more severe weirdness. Just watch your back, and I'll elaborate about what they saw when I see you in person."

"Roger that."

In the meanwhile of the meanwhile, Veronica, Becca, Dusty, and Rainy contacted the U.C. Berkeley astronomy faculty for a consultation about intergalactic planetarium tools befitting their new game plan. They made haste to get their stellar bearings. The trip home could wait, they said, as their transcendental affairs could be conducted as easily from the Bay Area as anywhere else. They were going to scry for the interstellar locations of the werewolves, mark the target regions on their Berkeley star charts, and project themselves into the cosmos to whip some ass.

"I have a hunch that last night's effort cleared the Milky Way of werewolves. But they still exist somewhere and under the proper circumstances, I'm sure they can easily return," Veronica said.

Point

With various actual reports of sky-high weirdness in the Bay Area, there was heightened nationwide buzz about Unidentified Flying Objects. The term is a misnomer pursuant to the incident in Oakland, because the craft was positively identified by the derby and their peace officer escorts. They knew it was a mother ship for a species of ambulatory space traveling sharks. But consequent to their individual lack of relevant historical knowledge that would be necessary for them to identify the amazing sky machine for what it was, the majority of witnesses used the stereotypical classification "unidentified."

Furthermore, strangely, the seas were burlier since Oakland's visit from the mother ship, off-season be damned, and West Coast surfers were out in great numbers. Moreover, while the visitors had been polite enough to keep a fairly stealthy disposition in the local waters, as it were, emergency dispatchers such as those in Tacoma, who were temporarily spared from calls about rampaging werewolves, now saw a spike in U.F.O. reports.

The universe is a big place and it was clear to the derby militia that they must shore-up their cartographic effort. For one thing, they decided the hunt should be relatively local, at least at first. Also, because Sol Charlie was incumbent as their protectorate and watchtower until further notice, they saw an immanent demand for constant local vigilance. Who else fit the job profile but them?

Rainy and Dusty fetched their specially requested, custom-made map materials from the Berkeley astronomy department: "Local intergalactic scale, about the size of our hotel room's tabletop," Dusty explained, whipping out the fancy paper tools. "And some nice deeper-space stuff too."

A late supper on Tuesday night found O.P.D.'s Sam Wilson back at the hunters' temporary headquarters. Crimson and Chapel were also nearby and willing. All stood around the kitchenette looking at the star charts on the table. Someone had shaded a rendering of the Local Solar Interstellar

Neighborhood with a highlighter pen, and scribbled the words "cleared" with a laundry marker.

"Our meditations and preliminary astral projections indicate that any bewitched space sharks are no longer locally preponderant," Becca said, "but, there could have been some problems at various nearby platforms, akin to what we had on local Sol. Such as Sirius, Tau Centari, Aldebaran, and Vega, et cetera."

"Talk about yer extra-local jurisdiction," detective Wilson barbed.

"Talk about it yeah but in truth it is right next door, chief, if not inside the house," she soberly responded. "Local-galactic is apparently free and clear of werewolves and co-opted space sharks. Relatively. For now. Anyway, we are all sensing something fishy, excuse the pun, farther out in slightly deeper reaches of the local keep. They are probably minor outposts amounting to potentially dangerous toeholds that need to be cleared, posthaste."

"Andromeda and Triangulum, like the Milky matriarch are clear at this time," she went on, "but outer space accommodates the tallest of shadows. Excepting some minor situations at limited or obscure locations, the Virgo III, Leo II, and Grus groups seem to be clear too. The Eridanus and Virgo clusters' orbits out in the Fornax also look clear."

"Beyond that, here are some more minor spots to look at, but canvassing outward into the known epoch, there are no evident large strongholds," she said. "But I suspect they can manifest in any backwater or other place that provides cover of darkness."

Rainy interjected: "Whether or not another crop of werewolves pops up on Sol will enlighten us about their potential tendencies of phenomenal redundancy, and of any delayed reaction to our organized opposition and eradication efforts. Tonight is another hunt, but it'll be more like a trip to the zendo than a rave."

Communications, Recruiting, and the Werewolf Net

After concluding a dinner of Oriental takeout in their hotel room, they spread out maps on the table top in the kitchenette and pinned them to the walls. No candles were lit, yet. For the purpose of dampening any unexpected fireworks on a hot L.Z., a geometrical landing strip was marked about the sliding glass window array at the room's north end, just in case anyone might need to quickly scuttle their astral projection for a blind emergency landing groundout back at the hotel.

Physically, they would remain in the

hotel room during the hunt. Wilson, Chapel, and Crimson were dispatched to post a general ground-zero lookout downstairs, passing the time in the bar of the lobby. In the event of any large scale physical dis-assimilation, gaping chasms, or earthly manifestations of dark armies, they would attempt to warn the hunters.

The Bay Area winter was setting in as showers and cooler temperatures replaced the sunshine that met the hunters at their arrival two days ago. The downstairs detachment headed for the elevator and the hunters made themselves comfortable among the couches in the suite's den.

Detective Thompson was taking advantage of the relative peace in his town, to catch up with his casework amid modifications to his department's operating protocol. He and lieutenant MacKinney sat in the break room at six Tuesday morning, thinking it over. The supernatural events were positively affecting the detective on the inside. The liquid speed was flowing from the office pot, but he had knocked off coffee along with booze and cigarettes cold turkey in recent weeks.

"As a point of order, when the tools of one's job include handcuffs, it has a tendency to reinforce an us-and-them view of the world," MacKinney editorialized. "Notwithstanding public agency in good faith and due process, during an arrest we are, by definition separating people from their civil liberties. Nevertheless we do try to be careful of hamfisted policies that get in the way of the ultimate and most fundamental goals of modern criminal justice such as rehabilitation and reintegration."

"Yeah, yeah, and it's safety first of course. But the main point is, the tendency toward such a natural default already makes police work resemble, in some very canny ways, the toils of zoologists," R. Thompson said. "On the other hand, there are times when certain unpopular methods are a necessity, we all know that. Take the shootout after the derby match, as an extreme example. Not much gray area there, but the point is, that situation was a far cry from court-ordered drug rehabilitation or the citizen's police academy. Scenes like that require an us-and-them perspective, e.g., me and the people versus violently rampaging werewolves. It is doubtless that a stitch in time saved more than nine lives that night."

"Such is the good judgment expected of peace officers, at all times," MacKinney said. "Your actions were exemplary that night, as they have been throughout this whole affair, and you know that."

"Well thanks, I'm just doing my job," the detective said, "the nature of which has changed. Our overall mission is changed and policy must reflect the difference. Dead bodies don't necessarily stay dead anymore. We've seen them turn into werewolves, or walk out of the ocean without a scratch, then go out for tacos. And monsters exist. We knew that before, but there are new ones now, shameless and mean. Some of them are from outer space. Luckily they've been pretty stupid so far, but even so they are organized and effective troublemakers. We must come to terms with the fact that future assaults will likely be more formidable."

"Suggestions?" the lieutenant quizzed.

"We put the good girls on the payroll for starters," the detective said, "and increase our collaboration with the other agencies we've worked with since the October eleventh killings, to maintain relations and coordinate our shared knowledge. Not just the locals but the posties including the Coast Guard. I just think it's worth lip service, if it seems like I'm stating the obvious."

"We will make those calls," said

MacKinney. "And you talk to our derby friends. Maybe they're amenable to part-time advisory roles. They don't seem to be particularly beholden to secular economics, so maybe they will do it on a volunteer basis. We could offer shiny badges in lieu of wages."

Denver Day

This Could be the Last Time

The maps turned out to have been effective as an anecdotal preparation tool for the galactic excursion, and they would also prove useful for post-excursion campaign progress analysis, however, they were weren't helpful during the actual mission since the hunters were light years away from their kitchenette table, time out of mind.

The team was dispatching itself to the Fornax Void for investigation of some anomalous, therefore suspicious, activity. Probably werewolves. Out there. The trip was meant to be a reconnaissance mission, barring circumstances on which they could easily reach consensus, on the fly, for deviation, e.g. strategic extermination operations.

They dimmed the lights, switched on low, ambient white noise, lit the candles, cranked up the hotel room's H.V.A.C. fan, crowded into one of the king-sized beds, covered themselves in the sheets and blankets, and began rhythmic chanting.

Veronica was the first to shine in at their destination. She parked herself in a long orbit of seven billion kilometers about a large, bright, relatively solitary blue sun. From her position in the system's planetary extremities, the blue star looked about the size of a small, bright, whitish-blue ball bearing.

Veronica's astral body was a highly

conductive, deep cold translucent metallic, rheologically waterlike configuration. She was a liquid metal strangely in essence both cold and hot. Catching ambient light from the local source, Veronica spun and pulsed a series of flashes at more distant points of light, which reported back with shimmers of their own. Then she shined her local host whose response was to connect with her, resonating with a subtle energy, warm and light.

She unfurled a beauty of a tail charged with a lovely amber glow, about five times the length of her main body. Veronica balled herself up into a spiky spiral, soaking up current through the subethereal medium with that tail, and willed the stream to arc with the star for several artful connections.

Pausing her frolicking, she directed her thoughts back to the hotel room, and moments later Becca, Dusty, and Rainy arrived, shimmering. They checkered in and out of the gravity wells of several close stars before parking themselves nearby Veronica. In airless space they could not speak out loud, but there was no need since the prescient stillness and relatively massive quiet emptiness of the surrounding cosmic medium facilitated cognitively audible communication outside of physical speech.

Dusty and Rainy had each made their tails about a mile long and were using them to spar which was showering the area with brilliant cascades of sparks. Becca was using her posterior appendage to hook up current with local planets, and her work in addition to making thick sheets of sparks, was generating multicolored lightning and low-range vibrations about the solar system. Meanwhile, floating peacefully, with her back to the friendly blue local, V. Roller was grokking out at the broadly swinging deeps of alien space.

We should get our mission-critical work done now. We can get back to this again later, thought Veronica, after a half hour of their cosmic diddling.

She's right. Let's put the hammer down, Becca concurred, pointing along a northerly vector with respect to their position, and furling her glowing orange tail, dripping sparks: They're that way, on the fourth rock in a nearby system of the same class as this blue one. Just a couple million kilometers away.

There are not many, maybe a hundred at most, Rainy observed.

Veronica: Then let's go. That's all for this entire region. If that platform were more crowded, we'd tread lighter, but it's just them camped alone, on some continent of old growth forest surrounded by a primordial ocean. First we'll barbecue their hairy asses from the air, then land to investigate.

Becca: Their inclination for darkness and solitude is good news. I would prefer not to encounter any densely populated werewolf colonies.

Rainy: Their presence on earth contradicted their M.O. of relative cosmic

Denver Day

solitude, Becca never say never.

Dusty: Whatever y'all. Let's go.

Behind huge but silent shock waves and ion plumes, each of the Rollers balled up and puddle-jumped next door to planet four.

Quark Beauté

www.ingramcontent.com/pod-product-compliance
Lightning Source LLC
Chambersburg PA
CBHW072029170626
46811CB00008B/3008